Dedicated to Margaret and her
parents Rebbecca and Enoch .....

Once upon a time there lived a family group of monkeys. There was Rebbecca the Mother. Also there was Enoch the Father. Finally there was Margaret the baby

daughter of the
family.

Margaret
was an
adventurous child
and she loved
exploring the
environment her
family lived in?

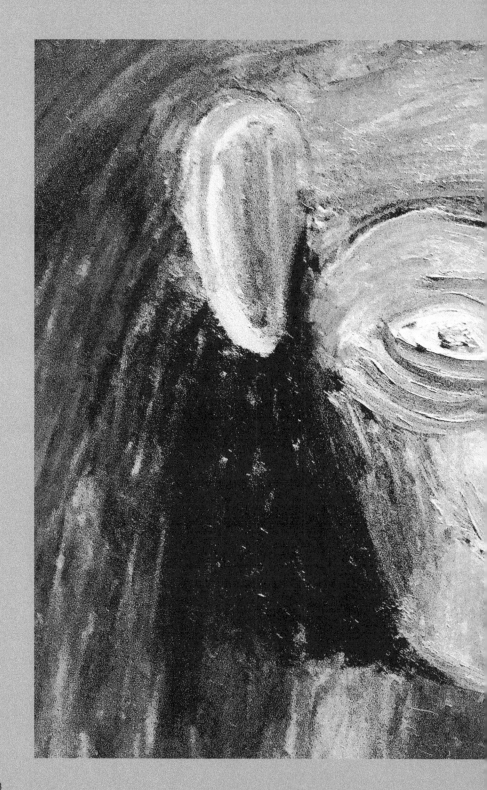

a mountainous part
of the country
called China or the
' Motherland '?

Rebbecca and
Enoch loved their
child Margaret very
much and made
sure she had
everything she

needed or wanted..

      Margaret
one day decided
that she wanted to
see the end of the
world and where
the land of China
ended. She had
heard the world

ended at ' The Great Wall of China'. So Margaret decided that she wanted to see the worlds end at ' The Great Wall of China'. Margaret did not think her parents would be concerned if she took a trip and a trip that she saw as the trip of a lifetime? So Margaret organized some food for her trip overland to ' The Great Wall of China '.

Margaret had to organize things for her trip to the end of the world in secret. She did not want her parents Rebbecca and Enoch to worry about her while she was away on her adventure?

The staple food for Margaret and her family was rice and bananas. In the region the family there was a plentiful supply of both staple foods?

To get to the

wall would take
Margaret a lot of
time traveling to it?
But Margaret was
very fit and also
very athletic for her
young age.

So
one night Margaret

began her journey to the end or edge of the known world? Margaret had heard from her friends all about ' The Great Wall of China ' , so in some ways she was prepared for what she would encounter at ' The Great Wall of China'

Margaret traveled many miles, mile after mile to get to her destination of ' The Wall'? Margaret was so looking forward

to seeing " The
Great Wall of China'
or the edge or end of
the known world?

When
Margaret gazed
upon it she was
suprised at her
emotional response
to being there. It had

a big impact upon
her emotionally. She
was at the edge or
end of the known
world. Would not
she have a tale to
tell her parents
Rebbecca and
Enoch. She missed
both of them very

much but she knew
she would be with
them soon?

But what a
tale Margaret would
have to tell them
all? She had gazed
upon the very edge
or end of the known

world and survived it?

Margaret wondered whether or not she should leave a marker for history at ' The Great Wall of China ' to say she had been there?

Margaret
wisely decided
against doing that?
She reasoned her
parents would not
be too happy with
her if she did that?

Margaret took
one last look over

the edge of ' The Great Wall of China' and decided to go home back to her parents? She hoped against all hope that they both would not be too upset with her for leaving secretly without their permission?

So Margaret made the perilous journey back to the mountains of China and her parents? She traveled mile, upon mile to get back to her home in the mountains and her waiting parents?

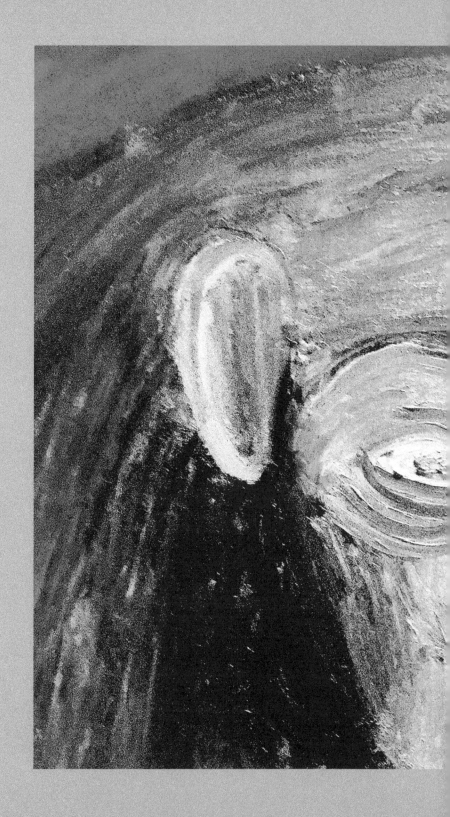

Rebbecca and Enoch Margaret's parents were overjoyed to have their daughter home again? They both could not believe the journey she had undertaken overland to ' The Great Wall of China ' the edge or end of the known world. They happily encouraged their daughter Margaret to tell them all about her journey. They were particularly interested in her description of the Wall. They hoped one day when Margaret was bigger to make the trip for themselves to ' The Great Wall of China'. It seemed to be a place they both needed to see?

Lightning Source UK Ltd.
Milton Keynes UK
UKHW022350300519
343606UK00002B/64/P